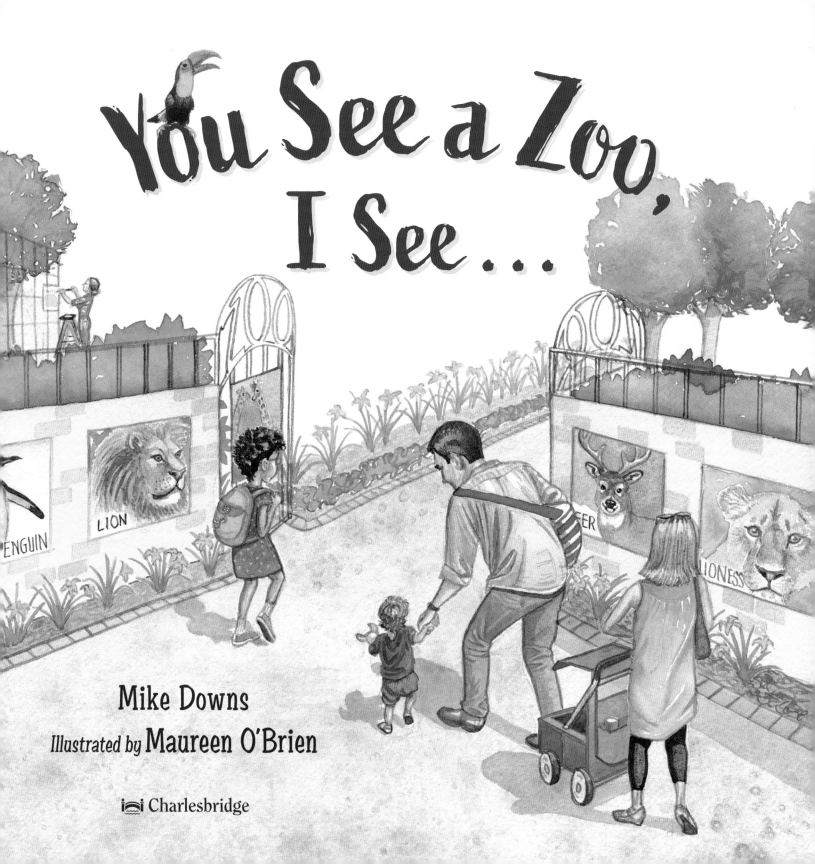

*For Victoria—my quirky, wonderful, loving
wife and companion, who chose to join me on
life's great adventure—M. D.*

*To Mary Bergin O'Brien and Vanessa Vassar,
who continue to inspire and challenge me
creatively, from beyond—M. O.*

Published by Charlesbridge
9 Galen Street, Watertown, MA 02472 • (617) 926-0329
www.charlesbridge.com

Printed in China
(hc) 10 9 8 7 6 5 4 3 2 1

Library of Congress Cataloging-in-Publication Data
Names: Downs, Mike, author. | O'Brien, Maureen
    (Illustrator), illustrator.
Title: You see a zoo, I see . . . / Mike Downs; illustrated by Maureen
    O'Brien.
Description: Watertown, M : Charlesbridge, [2022] | Audience: Ages
    3–7. | Audience: Grades K–1. | Summary: In rhyming text, a young
    narrator points out the family behaviors of different zoo animals,
    from crocodiles to lions—including her own mother, a zookeeper.
Identifiers: LCCN 2020051660 (print) | LCCN 2020051661 (ebook) |
    ISBN 9781623540999 (hardcover) | ISBN 9781632898555 (ebook)
Subjects: LCSH: Animal behavior—Juvenile fiction. | Zoo animals—
    Juvenile fiction. | Zoo keepers—Juvenile fiction. | Stories in rhyme.
    | Picture books for children. | CYAC: Stories in rhyme. | Animals—
    Habits and behavior—Fiction. | Zoo animals—Fiction. | Zoo
    keepers—Fiction. | LCGFT: Stories in rhyme. | Picture books.
Classification: LCC PZ8.3.D7542 Ys 2022 (print) | LCC PZ8.3.D7542
    (ebook) | DDC [E]—dc23
LC record available at https://lccn.loc.gov/2020051660
LC ebook record available at https://lccn.loc.gov/2020051661

Illustrations done in watercolor
Display type set in Active by Adam Ladd
Text type set in Berkeley © Adobe Systems
Scanning by Colourscan Print Co Pte Ltd, Singapore
Color separations and printing by 1010 Printing International Limited
    in Huizhou, Guangdong, China
Production supervision by Jennifer Most Delaney
Designed by Cathleen Schaad

The zoo! The zoo! We're here! We're here!
Elephants, crocodiles, ostriches, deer!
Kids of all ages rush to the door,
gawking at lions and penguins and more.

You see rowdy elephants.

Using trunks to squirt and spray,
everybody joins the fray.
Dropping, plopping with a thud,
twisting, rolling in the mud.

I see healthy kids at play.

Splashing in the murky pool
helps them keep their bodies cool.
Using mud to coat their skin
stops the ticks from getting in.

You see a scary crocodile.

Fearsome teeth and mighty jaws
match her sharp and pointy claws.
Her tail swishes side to side,
as bulging eyes begin to glide.

I see a protective mother.

Caring for her growing brood,
watching as they hunt for food.
Predators stay far away
when Mama Croc patrols the bay.

You see silly chimpanzees.

Leaping, jumping, dashing 'round,
climbing high above the ground.
Chasing, racing to and fro.
Chimps go fast and chimps go slow.

I see little ones at school.

Playing games is how they're taught
to run away and not get caught.
They also learn to pluck out fleas,
and build their nests aloft in trees.

You see lazy bats.

Tiny fur balls get their sleep,
hanging on with little feet.
Out of sight and safe from weather,
sometimes thousands roost together.

I see families at dinnertime.

Upside down they hang and squeal,
waiting for their evening meal.
Twilight brings them out to eat,
hunting for a tasty treat.

You see hiding ostriches.

Ostrich parents might be found,
heads together near the ground.
They keep a constant watchful eye.
They're very fast but never fly.

I see parents caring for their eggs.

In shallow holes and out of sight,
the eggs are turned by Dad at night.
Helping babies on the way,
Mama turns the eggs by day.

You see an angry lion.

Frightful roaring fills the air—
thunderous warnings meant to scare.
Those who hear him run and hide,
watching as he scans his pride.

I see a dad on the lookout.

The male lion stalks and prowls,
guarding home with rumbling growls.
Any stalkers still in place
quickly find him giving chase.

You see a zookeeper.

Very busy, on the run,
making sure her work is done.
Cleaning, feeding, checking up
on grizzly bear or jackal pup.

I see my mom.

Twice a week, she has a rule—
I get to help her after school.
I sweep the walk or peel some fruit,
and sometimes feed the baby newt!

Scary crocs and hungry bats,
lions, tigers, mighty cats.
Chimps that leap and climb in trees,
ostriches with backward knees.

That's the zoo you've always known . . .

. . . but when I see a zoo,
I see FAMILIES like our own!